Fantasy, Reality or Delusion?

Jyotsna Pathak is an 18-year-old, college-going, aspiring astrophysicist. She is a passionate poet who also enjoys fiction writing as much. Her stories reflect her dreams and perhaps fears, too. She has written various articles for her school magazine and likes to spend her free time watching football and horror movies. This is her debut work.

Connect with the author at
Instagram: @jyotsnapathakk

Jyotsna Pathak, at the young age of eighteen, shows considerable literary talent. Her short stories provide an intriguing and enticing window into the workings of a sensitive mind.

> —**Pavan K. Varma**, author, former diplomat and former Member of Parliament (Rajya Sabha)

A most mystifying collection of stories and poems of a budding author whose work would leave you gasping for breath and asking for more. A rare talent we should all look out for. She is bound to go places.

> —**Neeraj Kumar**, author and former Commissioner of Delhi Police

Jyotsna Pathak clearly has a flair for writing both poetry and short stories. They have a lyrical quality about them and, at the same time, are deeply philosophical, with an intriguing air of mystery. She has a great career ahead of her as a writer.

> —**Rahul Singh**, former Editor-in-Chief, *Reader's Digest India*

Fantasy, Reality or Delusion?

A Collection of Short Stories and Poems

JYOTSNA PATHAK

Published by
Rupa Publications India Pvt. Ltd 2024
7/16, Ansari Road, Daryaganj
New Delhi 110002

Sales Centres:
Bengaluru Chennai
Hyderabad Jaipur Kathmandu
Kolkata Mumbai Prayagraj

Copyright © Jyotsna Pathak 2024

This is a work of fiction. Names, characters, places and incidents are either the product of the author's imagination or are used fictitiously and any resemblance to any actual person, living or dead, events or locales is entirely coincidental.

All rights reserved.
No part of this publication may be reproduced, transmitted or stored in a retrieval system, in any form or by any means, electronic, mechanical, photocopying, recording or otherwise, without the prior permission of the publisher.

P-ISBN: 978-93-5702-927-8
E-ISBN: 978-93-5702-803-5

First impression 2024

10 9 8 7 6 5 4 3 2 1

The moral right of the author has been asserted.

Printed in India

This book is sold subject to the condition that it shall not, by way of trade or otherwise, be lent, resold, hired out or otherwise circulated, without the publisher's prior consent, in any form of binding or cover other than that in which it is published.

To my beloved grandfather,
the late Dr Bindeshwar Pathak
(2 April 1943–15 August 2023).
May his blessings always inspire me
to do the best for the world.

CONTENTS

1. Au Claire de la Lune — 1
2. Atonement — 5
3. The Tipping House — 11
4. Staying Up — 16
5. Hallucination — 20
6. Agenda — 28
7. Poison Tree — 36
8. What a Beautiful Rose! — 40
9. I Was All Over Her — 61
10. Paradise — 71
11. Oh, Dear Jamie — 76
12. Xoxo, the Antique Burglar — 79
13. Heist of Lives — 103
14. Runaway — 106
15. Fantasy — 117

1

AU CLAIRE DE LA LUNE

Humanity under a blanket,
Flourishes.
A blanket with seamless seams,
Sewn together by celestials.

The universe brought together by secrecy,
A secret unknown to all.
Rigid in all its sense,
While pliant as a rubber ball.

What do we know about the place we live in?
A place we have inhabited since the dawn of time.
Apart from its infinite nature,
Spooky as it is sublime.

FANTASY, REALITY OR DELUSION?

I look up at the sky and see the moon,
While bathing in its incessant light.
Encapsulating its divine presence,
Through my tiny, insignificant eyes.

I capture a picture through the means I procure,
A scenery my eyes can never forget.
Can never dare to speak in front of the divine,
In front of which humanity can only fret.

An extensive deity immeasurable by far,
In front of which our existence feels small.
Small as an ant who can't understand,
The meaning of life, why we sacrifice it all.

The universe remembers the sins and the aid,
The dry rivers which now thrive again.
It remembers the vast progression of humanity,
And even the poor man's pain.

It remembers and remembers,
A huge storage unit if you may.
And at the centre of it all,
Us humans we lay.

FANTASY, REALITY OR DELUSION?

The insignificance of our civilization,
Now comes into play.
When the possibility of our universe being endless,
Brings forth a whole new display.

It is considered stupid to talk to a rat,
Try to feed it intellectual knowledge.
While we humans, rats, in front of the universe,
Wait for it to feed us its secret like porridge.

The universe doesn't care,
Nor will it ever do.
I contemplate if I'll ever know what is and what is not,
While sitting *Au Claire de la Lune.*

2

ATONEMENT

It was sometime around midnight. I was on my way home from a party. It was a little chilly; nonetheless, I was standing on the platform waiting for my train to arrive at the station. My house was just three stations away.

I was barely in my senses, and everything seemed so foggy. I was a little too intoxicated that day. Soon after I had puked, I felt better, but I was still very drunk. I remember things in fragments. My memory is not the best. Moreover, I was barely conscious.

After I puked, I decided to call it a night. A friend dropped me off at the train station, and I insisted that I was okay to travel the rest of the way home by myself. I really wasn't, but I didn't want to drag him away from

FANTASY, REALITY OR DELUSION?

the party. Doing so would ruin my reputation, and I would be termed a loser.

I sat on a bench waiting for the train to arrive. The station was more or less deserted but for a peculiar man in a top hat sitting across from me, and even he had just arrived. I call him peculiar because if I remember correctly, he was wearing a tuxedo, which, at the time, I found strange for some reason.

Soon enough, the train arrived. There were only three passengers: me, the peculiar man and a little boy. I sat down next to the little boy, not interested in making any conversation because I was not feeling up to it.

'Will you play with me?' the little boy said with a teddy bear in his hand, reaching out to me. 'Sorry, kid. Go find your mom to play with or something,' I said. The kid kept insisting, 'Please, please, please play with me.'

I should mention now that I have a short temper, so I get annoyed very quickly.

The train's window was open, so I got up—wobbling from side to side, hardly able to stand still—took the child's bear and threw it outside. He got up on the seat and screamed, 'NO, MY TEDDY!' as he saw it fly away and land on the train tracks. I let out a giggle, unable to believe what I had just done.

The child then proceeded to do something I never

FANTASY, REALITY OR DELUSION?

would've imagined anyone could do for a mere teddy bear. He jumped out of the same train window while it was still moving.

I immediately got up to look at what had happened, but the night was pitch black, and I couldn't see anything except mist and thick fog.

The next stop was mine, and I was barely in my senses to process what had happened. I just wanted to forget about it and go home. Suddenly, the peculiar guy sitting across from me stood up. *Oh no, he just witnessed the whole thing*, I thought to myself. What I couldn't comprehend at the time was why he had sat through that whole ordeal in absolute silence.

He came and sat down next to me. He lifted his hat only to reveal bloodshot eyes. 'You will atone for your sins just like I atoned for mine,' he said staring right into my eyes with a frightening look on his face.

Scared out of my wits, I stood up. After a dizzy spell, I fell and lost consciousness. When I woke up, I was in a hospital with my parents and siblings standing around me with worried looks on their faces. I asked them what had happened. They said the cops had found me lying unconscious on the ground with a dead butterfly lodged in my throat. They thought I was dead, but when they checked, I still had a pulse.

ATONEMENT

After a while, the doctor left me alone with my mom, dad and two brothers. Each of them had something different to say to me. They kept screaming at me, but my mind was focused on only one thing: what had happened last night?

'I have to get out of here,' I said while trying to crawl out of the bed. My family insisted I stay in the hospital, but I had to figure out what had happened. I hurried to the train station. It was around four in the afternoon.

There were a lot of people on the platform, and a group of teens was talking about something among themselves. I did not mean to be nosy, but I overheard the word 'teddy', which intrigued me, so I went up to them.

'I didn't mean to eavesdrop, but do you guys mind telling me what you were talking about?' I asked. One of the girls standing there said, 'There's a rumour around these areas about this train station. About 40 years ago, a psychopath escaped a mental asylum and killed a young boy on a train that departed from here. After killing the little boy, he killed himself too. His mom was devastated and lost her mind. In the end, she was admitted to a hospital where she went crazy and eventually took her own life. The killer had left a note with the little boy's teddy that said, "You will atone for your sins," in the same seat where he had murdered the boy.'

Hearing those words sent a chill down my spine, and I couldn't move for a second. As I looked up, I saw the same old man with bloodshot eyes looking at me and waving from a train car. My heart started racing, and I screamed, 'SOMEONE GET ME AWAY FROM HERE, SOMEONE PLEASE!'

Suddenly, a butterfly came out of nowhere and found its way down my oesophagus. It lodged itself inside my throat till I choked and fell to my untimely death in front of the group of teens who couldn't react quickly enough to save me.

All of you reading, don't be frightened. That's what such entities feed on—fear.

Don't worry. Even you will atone for your sins one day.

3

THE TIPPING HOUSE

Far away in a land so mystic,
That sometimes it isn't land at all.
On occasion, when the Earth's crust melts like lava,
Turning into a beautiful waterfall.

Through the months of May to June,
Though no one has experienced this change first-hand,
A waterfall flourishes with a river underneath it,
Leaving no proof of the existence of land.

FANTASY, REALITY OR DELUSION?

Floating on this river are tiny houses,
With families drowning in oh so much stress.
Because the house doesn't sustain weight,
When the distribution is unequal and messed.

The locals find the families eerie,
Wondering how they live inside
Having to worry about weight being equally distributed
At all times, with not a gram to slide.

Legend says these families are a legacy,
A legacy of the pride of the land.
The dozen men who found the place,
And built it from a mere grain of sand.

In May, the houses move along the river,
Passing by the fields of corn and flower
But they disappear in the month of June,
Leaving behind a taste so sour.

The locals don't mind this spectacle,
Bearing it because of the stories they learned.
The stories told by generations of elders,
Speaking about the war that formed.

FANTASY, REALITY OR DELUSION?

On a bright sunny day in May,
When the corn was ripe and the flowers were blooming
An ambush out of nowhere erupted,
With force that could have been dooming.

But the dozen men worked harder and harder,
Till they had no option left,
Other than to rely on the universe,
Rely on destiny to repair their cleft.

In two days, a loud noise was heard,
Bringing the villagers up on their feet
To discover something so marvellous
A waterfall out of nowhere which tasted
oh so sweet.

It swept away the enemy and the camps they laid,
Leaving behind tents that floated on the water
In which the men set up their homes,
To raise their own son and daughter.

The houses maintain peace,
Or so they say
Some say it's a curse on the men
Reparation for the tricks they play.

THE TIPPING HOUSE

A curse passed on to their families,
Punished for the sins they committed.
Rumour has it the men put to death innocent prisoners,
And deceived the villagers, lying about the acquitted.

An escape from the enemy who found out,
Running away to the land with stolen money.
The money they earned killing innocent people,
All for the rich to further fatten their tummy.

All in all, the river flourishes,
May it be full of sin or harmony.
The tipping houses appear every summer,
Along with the waterfall generating its euphony.

4

STAYING UP

I was dreaming.

It was around one in the afternoon, and I was walking around an unfamiliar neighbourhood.

It was an American neighbourhood, whereas I live in India. Apparently, I lived there according to my subconscious mind.

I was feeling really low and stressed for some reason. I was walking around and just passing by tall palm trees when I saw one of my friends walking towards me.

He came up to me and asked me why I looked so tense. It was because of my anxiety that had suddenly started acting up for no reason.

I told him I was not tense and tried walking past

him but stopped right as he asked me if I wanted a little something to calm me down. I walked back to him.

He handed me a half-black and half-white pill. He said it would help me calm down. Being naive and desperate and wanting to get rid of this anxiety, I took it.

He said, 'Don't you want to thank me?' So I thanked him. He said, 'You owe me one.' I bid him goodbye and made my way home.

On the way home, I started to feel a little dizzy but thought nothing of it. As soon I reached home, my parents asked me if I had taken any kind of drugs. I immediately refused but wondered if my friend had actually given me a drug.

They held my palm, and the black part of the pill was still there. It was bizarre as I had already consumed the entire pill. How could it possibly be there?

They asked me what it was. I shrugged it off as something I did not know about. I went back to my room where I saw my friend sitting on my bed.

'Don't you want to thank me?' he said. I went over to slap him only for him to disappear into thin air. I collapsed. My palms were all sweaty, but I was feeling cold. I could barely open my eyes, but I did make out some words on the ceiling, 'Don't you want to thank me?', before fainting.

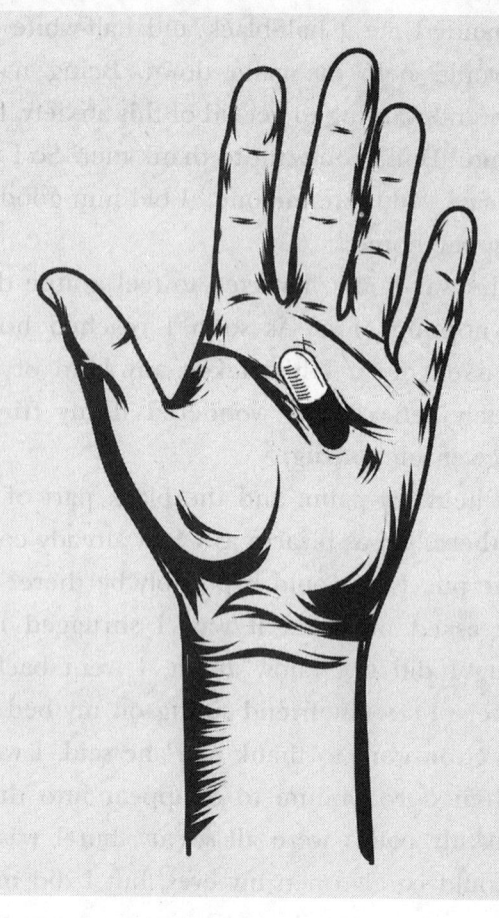

STAYING UP

Before I knew it, I was strapped to the bed in a hospital. A nurse came in. I asked her what was happening and where I was. She kept whispering something that I could not make out. I asked her to speak up and stop whispering creepily. She looked at me with fierce, bright red eyes and asked, 'Don't you want to thank me?'

She then took a pill that looked exactly like the one I had taken before and shoved it down my throat with her bare hands. I felt faint. I could not speak. I could feel myself losing my breath, and I wasn't able to do anything about it. I did not feel strong. I could not hold on any more. And yet, I didn't feel like I was dying. I felt like I was transforming.

As I fell to the ground, feeling like an entirely new being and feeling my memory slowly fade, the nurse transmogrified into my friend, smiled and said, 'You owed me one. Now you don't owe me anything. Don't you want to thank me?'

I woke up in a sweat even though I was sleeping with the fan on. I sat up and extended my hand towards the water bottle on my bedside table. As I gulped down some water, I could hear a faraway voice ringing in my head, saying, 'Thank me. You owe me.'

5

HALLUCINATION

I was at the airport with my parents on my way back to my home town. We were in New Zealand for a holiday, but sadly, it had come to an end.

My mom and I were standing in the check-in line waiting for our turn to check our luggage in and pick up our tickets. The line wasn't that long, but annoyingly enough, the person at the counter was taking way longer than they should've.

I was not paying much attention to the chaos around me. Instead, I had AirPods in my ears, and I was listening to sweet old heavy metal, happily minding my own business.

I was waiting for my dad to come back from getting

HALLUCINATION

my mom some coffee so I could beg him for a little more time on holiday because trust me, I was in no mood to go back home.

Suddenly, I heard such a loud sound that it pierced through my AirPods, almost as if their existence had ceased for a second. Soon after, part of the airport collapsed because of the weird and horribly loud whistle and sent rubble flying all over the place. It knocked me and my mom down, but thankfully, we weren't hurt.

I didn't really want to leave my mom alone, but I told her to find shelter while I went looking for my dad. A million thoughts raced through my head, and most of them weren't happy ones.

I was worried something had happened to my dad and that I would end up not finding him. I couldn't get that thought out of my head as much as I didn't want to accept it.

I was also stressing about the fact that I had left my mom alone and tasked her with finding some shelter without any help. What if something happened to her too? I saw my future flashing before my eyes while I continued searching for my dad.

I reached the entrance of the airport, and I saw a lady and a man fighting with something that looked quite like a sword. It did not take me long to realize that the man

FANTASY, REALITY OR DELUSION?

fighting the lady was my dad. Five men and three women were huddled behind my dad. Hiding behind a piece of rubble, I was scared for my life and confused as to what was happening. A million questions were running through my head. Why was my dad fighting this random woman? Since when does my dad know how to use a sword? Why does he own a sword in the first place, and why is this the first time I've seen it?

My eyes were glued to the fight, and I was paying attention to every little detail. All of a sudden, something out of the ordinary happened. My dad tapped his sword twice, and it started glowing with a hue of neon blue. As he hit the woman with his sword, it was as though all the life in her eyes was being sucked out.

But that was not the end of it. Another woman dressed in an outlandish attire with a sword that was glowing pink came along. While I was peeping at the fight, forgetting to be discreet with my detective work, I did not notice that the people standing behind my father had become aware of my existence and that I was looking at the fight with a huge amount of interest. Essentially, what I did not realize was that they had noticed me.

As they approached me, they caught me off guard. I jumped backwards and instantly took out the pocketknife I always carried with me.

HALLUCINATION

'Who are you guys? How do you know my father, and what do you want with me? Stay away from me!' I screeched as though my life depended on it.

'Oh, little lady, calm down. We're on your dad's side,' one of the men approaching me said. 'How do you know which one is my dad? I never told you who he was,' I said, taking a step backwards for fear of my life.

'I mean, there's only one man there fighting a woman, so wouldn't it be insanely weird if she's your dad? It's quite obvious. Anyway, even if you don't know us, we know you very well,' a peculiar little woman said, giggling at my stupidity.

'Why should I trust you? How do I know you're not lying to me and this isn't all part of some conspiracy?' I said.

'You had a teddy bear named Ciara when you were five years old. It was pink in colour, and initially, you hated it because pink is your least favourite colour, but you grew to love it, and it became your favourite stuffed toy. Now, tell me, would a stranger know such stuff?' the man said, giggling a little. I was baffled, but what was the matter with these people giggling like idiots? Also, how did they know such stuff? Only my parents and closest friends knew about Ciara and how much she meant to me.

FANTASY, REALITY OR DELUSION?

'Here, take this,' the peculiar little woman said, handing me a sword and something that looked a lot like playing cards—two of them.

'Even if you all are my dad's friends, I need to go find my mom. I left her alone, and I don't feel too great about it,' I said unnervingly.

'Kid, even if you don't know us, we do know you. Your mom is safe in one of our hiding spots. When we take you there later, you might even find some familiar faces around,' the man said.

By the time we finished having this conversation, the fight between my dad and the weird woman was over. He and the rest of the people standing behind him made their way over to me. At this point I was so horrified that I had tears in my eyes, and I was on the brink of crying like crazy.

'Come on, sweetheart. Let's go,' my dad said, reaching for my hand. I grabbed his hand as he threw a playing card down at the ground and it exploded. In the blink of an eye, I was in a peculiar-looking place. It looked like a train, but something was off about it. It wasn't just a train; it was situated on a huge rock or something. I let go of my dad's hand to look down over the edge of the rock and saw that we were floating in the sky.

HALLUCINATION

'What the hell?' I exclaimed loudly. 'Mind your language, little one,' my dad said walking towards me. 'Dad, what is all this? How did we get here? How is this rock floating, and why is there a train attached to it?' I screamed in confusion.

'Don't worry. You'll find out soon enough. I'm sorry. I have to go, but I promise I'll be back soon,' he said as he threw another playing card on the ground and disappeared before I could interrupt.

As he disappeared, I noticed a familiar face at the doorway of the train. It was one of my school friends. 'What are you doing here?' I said more confused than ever, trying to process everything that was happening.

'Oh great! You made it. Come over here. The view is so beautiful,' he said, grabbing my hand and pulling me to the edge.

As I looked down, I saw a breathtaking view of the city. 'Is this real? Am I dreaming? All of this seems too complicated to be real, but it still feels like reality,' I said.

'My friend, don't let anything fool you. Everything you've seen today is real. But if you start doubting whether it's real or not, you might get sucked into the villain's lair. He feeds on the fear and doubt that lurks in people's minds and transports them to a reality very different from ours, which could prove to be fatal and inescapable.'

HALLUCINATION

As soon as my friend said that, he dissolved into thin air, and I felt someone tugging at my shoulder. It was my mom waking me up. 'Come on. Wake up. It's time for our flight,' she scolded.

As I woke up, I was confused. I was back in the airport, but instead of it being demolished, I was sitting in a lounge with my head on a pillow. *Was it a dream?* I wondered. Everything about it felt so real. It felt like it wasn't just a dream. Was I trapped in the villain's lair? Or was it all really a dream? I guess I will never know.

6

AGENDA

It was a lovely day outside. It had rained the night before, so a chilly wind was overpowering the scorching July heat, the kind that prickled your skin.

I was walking down a street trying to get to work on time. With earphones in place, I was blissfully listening to music and wasn't paying much attention to my surroundings.

The street, being quite popular amongst the locals and having a lot of famous restaurants, was chaotic. One of my favourite pizza joints was on the same street. I crossed it every day on my way to work.

There was a shady-looking alley just next to where the pizza joint was. It was a shortcut to my workplace, which I rarely took as it was really strange and kind of creepy if you ask me. But on this fine day, I was running late for work, so I decided to take that alley.

I wasn't really bothered by the thought of crossing it. I had crossed it many times before. I, once again, was not aware of my surroundings; instead, I was lost in my music.

Suddenly, two women appeared before me out of nowhere. One grabbed my arms while the other put a cloth over my face doused in what felt like chloroform because soon after, I lost consciousness.

When I awoke, I was in a room with grey walls. I was strapped to a chair with something that felt like an aeroplane seat belt and wrist restraints, and I had a kind of helmet on my head. There was no one in the room as far as I could see. Moreover, the room was dead silent to the point I could hear my own heartbeat.

My neck was also cuffed to the chair, so I couldn't lift my head to look at what was around me. I was seriously questioning my life choices at this moment.

Why did I wake up late that morning? If I wasn't a lazy brat, I would never be in this situation.

About an hour passed, and just as I was starting to get consumed by my own thoughts, I heard a door open. Someone walked up to me; it was a man. His head hovered above me. He looked to be 30–40 years old,

FANTASY, REALITY OR DELUSION?

and was wearing glasses and a weird kind of transparent shower cap on his head.

He was also wearing a lab coat over what looked like a nurse's uniform. The man was looking kind of funny if you ask me, but it wasn't strategically smart to laugh at my kidnapper.

Forgetting he was the one holding me hostage and not the other way around, I accidentally chuckled as I saw him. Not that I would hold someone hostage, but you get what I mean.

'What is so funny that it made you laugh? You're being held hostage, and instead of being scared, you're laughing? And I thought I was a psychopath,' he said. I mumbled under the tape that was plastered over my mouth. The man ripped it off like a band-aid.

'Ouch. That was not so nice now, was it? Well, it's not my fault you're a funny-looking man. Either way, I know you're going to kill me, so why be scared when I can come to terms with it? I already know what to expect and what the future holds. It's going to happen anyway even if I don't want it to happen.'

'Miss, you're mistaken. If you really think our main objective is to kill you, you are way off.'

'Who else is working with you?'

'What makes you think I'm not working alone?'

AGENDA

'I mean, you said "our", so clearly, there are other people you're working with. Anyway, if your objective is not to kill me, then what is it?'

'Well, do you inform a hen before taking its eggs? And even if you did, would it understand why? Exactly. I'll be back shortly,' he said rushing out of the door.

'No, WAIT!' I screamed, desperately wanting answers, but he had already left. I spent hours in there, doing nothing, chained to the chair. I tried to scream for help, but there was an echo, which made me believe the room was soundproofed.

For a minute, I genuinely thought I'd go insane or something. Spending hours and hours alone gave me time to consider and play out every single crazy outcome in my mind and think about all the different possibilities.

The first question in my mind was what was their objective? Second, who was this man working with, and how many people were involved in this? Third, did they choose me specifically or was I just someone random they chose to pick off the street?

I could go on and on about all the thoughts running through my mind, but there was one that occupied the most space inside my head. Was I going to make it out alive?

Truth is, I'm a lonely person. I was raised by a single

father who had died five years ago. I have no clue who my mother was because my father never really talked about her. I was a single child. My father was never in contact with his family—he hated their guts—so no relatives. I had a few acquaintances at my workplace, but that was all they were, acquaintances. I wasn't exactly social and enjoyed my own company. I had never even been in a proper relationship.

So basically, even if I wound up being dead in some shady alley, no one would miss me. I wasn't exactly scared of dying. It would've eventually caught up with me anyway. Everyone dies.

I was all up in my head when I heard some indistinct whispers. It was like a group of people talking, but I could not make out what they were saying or where the sound was coming from. Suddenly, I heard the door creak open again, but this time it was accompanied by the sound of the click of heels.

I tried to turn my head to the side just as a blonde lady approached me. She was wearing gloves and was in the same get-up as the guy who was here before. The only exception was that her shower cap was not transparent; it was pink and opaque instead.

'Are you here to kill me just because your other guy friend couldn't bring himself to do it? Is he that soft?'

AGENDA

I said to her. She said nothing but just stared at me, wide-eyed.

She picked up something from a table kept beside the chair I was strapped in. I couldn't see it, but I just assumed it was a table. The lady put her finger to her lips to create a shushing motion.

'Are you dumb? I mean, can you not speak? What are you shushing me for?'

'Your words mean nothing, so you should stay quiet,' she said.

'What do you mean my words mean nothing? Am I not human? I have the same rights as you, don't I? Even if you don't kill me, I will die eventually sometime in the future. That still won't change the fact that I am human and my words matter. No matter what you say, even if there is no one to investigate my de—' I stopped.

It was foolish of me to tell her no one would investigate my death if I died. However much it might be true, it wouldn't help me in my current situation.

'Young child, we know everything about you. We specifically chose you because we knew no one would investigate your death to the point where they discover the truth,' she said as she held a syringe in her hand.

FANTASY, REALITY OR DELUSION?

'Your words don't matter because no one except me will ever hear them again,' she said pushing the syringe into the skin under my elbow.

'WHAT KIND OF A DERANGED HUMAN BEING DOES SUCH A HEINOUS THING?' I screamed as I struggled to get out.

What was this? What was in the syringe? Was I going to die? 'We just wanted to make an example…' Before she could finish her sentence, I blacked out.

When I woke up, I was standing in the middle of a

street I didn't recognize. Just a few seconds later, I fell to my feet. I could hear my heart thumping and I was running out of breath. I tried to scream for help, but nothing came out. As I took my last breath, I could see people running to help me. This was it. Suddenly everything went black, and I never woke up.

The Daily Journal
Sunday 12/09/2045
Woman Mysteriously Dissolves into Liquid in the Middle of Street

The latest spectacle we hear is that civilians on their way to work witnessed the most unnatural and brutal death of a woman dissolving into liquid and falling down the drain. Scientists are currently working on a hypothesis of how such a thing is humanly possible. This seems to be a warning from a well-known political party and is to be taken as a sign of war. Stay in your homes, folks. Stay safe.

7

POISON TREE

Once upon a time, when I was living in the countryside with my parents, I planted a seed in my backyard. I wanted to grow a tree. My backyard was not technically a backyard but more like a little garden leading to a huge forest.

I was always fond of nature and its beauty, even as a kid. For the next eighteen years, till I moved to college for my degree, I used to water it every day on my way back from school.

Soon enough, it matured into a large and beautiful oak tree. I admired it a lot. It was mystical and enigmatic in a mesmerizing manner. I used to imagine that one day, it would turn into a magnificent, huge, colourful tree

with a lot of different birds and animals surrounding it, especially squirrels, which were my favourite.

I also believed Moon-Face and his friends from my favourite book series, *The Magic Faraway Tree*, would live there and go on different magical adventures every day. If I was lucky to stumble upon their lair, maybe one day I would be able to go on an adventure in a faraway fantastical world too.

Soon I left for college. I was extremely confident my oak tree would be gorgeous by the time I came back.

I spent my days thinking about my oak tree and hoping I would get to see it soon. I was eager to get my medical degree and go back home. I spent around ten years studying, still as eager as ever to go see my old oak tree.

After completing my studies, I finally decided to go back to my old house. My parents had moved out a few years ago to go live in the city, but they had not sold the house yet.

When I reached my old home, I saw that it was covered in climbing vines. My immediate response was to run to my backyard.

The picture in front of me left a frown on my face. There I saw my beautiful oak tree, covered in layers of mistletoe. The mistletoe had drained the life out of the tree, imbibing the nutrients and water from the tree to survive.

My beloved tree, almost dead now, was nowhere close to the image I had had in my head. My precious oak tree, I'm sorry I couldn't save you.

In our lives, we come across different types of people every day, some caring, some toxic. Our inexperience and love compel us to hold on to a toxic person and blind us towards how much they hurt us. The person feasts on our kindness and love until it finally empties us and leaves behind a broken soul. A toxic person robs their victim of their happiness, leaving them alone with their own thoughts.

Not everyone is toxic; not everyone is nice; not everyone can overcome tough situations; and not everyone knows how to handle every situation perfectly. In the end, learning is a part of life, and every bad situation helps you learn something new and improve your judgement.

Learning how to take bad incidents in a positive way and identifying people with bad intentions is crucial in this world, but it's not as easy as it seems. It's easy to say something, but implementation is difficult.

Don't let the mistletoe ruin your oak tree.

8

WHAT A BEAUTIFUL ROSE!

When I was ten years old and living in my old house, I didn't have a lot of friends. I would usually stay by myself and waste away my days on the swing. My parents were never really around; they were always busy with their work. The only person in my house except me would be my servant.

The swing in my house was attached to a tall tree. It was so tall that I would have to ask someone to lift me just so I could sit on it. I could see pretty much everything around my house from up there. I would spend my time swinging, waiting for a car to appear. As soon as one appeared, I would wish it stopped by my house, but it usually didn't.

FANTASY, REALITY OR DELUSION?

I would wait for hours for my parents to come back, but they would only return after I had fallen asleep. They would leave with me as I left for school. I didn't really see them much; I don't know why they thought that would be healthy for a ten-year-old.

Anyway, I didn't mind because I preferred the solitude. Besides, it was not like I was always alone. I had exactly three friends who lived around my house.

One was my neighbour, Aliya; one lived across the street from me, Rahul; and one lived at the end of the street, Jo. We all were really good friends and hung out a lot. Even though they all meant the same to me, considering I was a child at the time, I was inclined towards Jo a teeny, tiny bit.

Maybe it was because our situations were the same. Jo was as rich as one can be. Both his parents worked full-time as architects and were mostly out of town for meetings and projects. They didn't pay much attention to him either.

Jo had an elder sister whom he loved more than anyone, but even she moved abroad to complete her higher studies. He would get lonely a lot, not much different from the situation I was dealing with, though I would not like to compare.

I liked being alone, but being alone and being lonely

WHAT A BEAUTIFUL ROSE!

are completely different things, and I sure as hell was lonely. These three friends of mine were the people I cared about most in the world. We basically grew up together. We would play games, watch movies, read stories, have sleepovers, go to parties, study for finals and do many other things together. They were like the siblings I never had.

These small things and spending time with my friends made me forget about the pathetic life I had and my parents who couldn't care less about me. I would have bad days, exceptionally bad days, and being with my friends would instantly cheer me up. Those were the best days of my life.

When I was around sixteen, I started developing feelings for Jo. It was a little unusual considering we had the same friend circle.

I initially decided to keep it a secret, but then the day finally came, the day I had dreaded for years. I was going to move away. I hadn't told my friends yet. I didn't know how to tell them. What would I say to them? How would they react? I didn't know what to do.

I was most worried about telling Jo. I was worried about how he'd react. I didn't want to move away; I didn't want to move away *at all*, but I didn't have an option.

FANTASY, REALITY OR DELUSION?

Oh, good lord. What am I going to do? I thought to myself. The next day, I got up an hour before I had to so I could go to Jo's house to tell him. I called Aliya and Rahul to Jo's too but thirty minutes before school. I wanted to tell Jo alone.

∽

I couldn't sleep properly the previous night; all I could think about was what to say. No right words came to mind. I kept thinking about what would happen to our friendship after I moved. Would we stay in touch? Would we still remain friends? This would've been easy if I was moving to another part of town, but I was moving to another city altogether.

This was annoyingly difficult. What should I do? I woke up incredibly tired but was still wide awake and feeling fresh for some reason.

I ate a little breakfast, even though I was not really hungry. I would be leaving the people I cared about the most in a week; I was on the verge of breaking down.

I barely held myself together as my mother came over to me. 'Why aren't you eating, sweetie?' she asked in a weary tone. She had never ever asked me this before. I think that was mainly because I always ate enough food, and on time, at least in front of my parents. They rarely

WHAT A BEAUTIFUL ROSE!

saw me, so they had no idea what my eating habits were.

Because of the mood I was in, my mom daring to ask me that pissed me off.

'You've never cared about me before, so why care now? Is it because you lost your job and now you have to stay at home with me? Or is it because you feel guilty that you're making us move a thousand miles away just because your boss fired you? Now I have to leave my friends who actually care about me to go away with you and Dad who don't even acknowledge my existence. Quit the act; it isn't fooling anyone,' I said with tears streaming down my face.

Slapping both my hands on the table, I got up and kicked my chair. Before she could say anything to worsen my already ruined mood, I grabbed my bag and ran out of the door, banging it shut as I left, frantically trying to wipe the tears off my face as my heart shattered into a million pieces.

I walked all the way to the end of the street to Jo's house. Before I could ring the doorbell, someone opened the door and a familiar face emerged with a screwdriver in her hand.

'Oh, hi Tara! It's so nice to see you after so long.' It was Jo's sister.

'Oh my god, what a pleasant surprise!' I exclaimed. As

FANTASY, REALITY OR DELUSION?

I went in for a hug, I saw Jo making his way to the door.

'Tara, what are you doing here? You're almost forty-five minutes early. I haven't even brushed my teeth yet.'

'Oh Jo, I'm so sorry. I had to talk to you about...' Before I could finish my sentence, I could see a gleaming smile on Jo's face. He had really missed his sister, and he looked as happy as ever. I didn't know if I wanted to ruin his mood by telling him about my moving to another city.

'What happened, Tara? Where are you lost?' he said, giggling and waving his hand in front of my face to get my attention.

'I was thinking about something. Jo, can I talk to you alone for a second?' I asked.

'I'll leave you two to it while I go fix this light bulb,' Jo's sister said as she excused herself. My face dropped suddenly.

'What happened, Tara? Is something wrong?'

'I don't know how to tell you this.' I hesitated a little.

'I'm moving.'

His smiling face suddenly turned serious.

'Are you joking? Is this a prank or something? Because it isn't funny,' he said, smiling a little. His smile changed back into a frown as my facial expression remained stagnant.

'Why? When did this happen? When did you find out?' He started bombarding me with questions.

'Do Aliya and Rahul know? Where are you moving to? Will you be visiting?' He grew more and more frantic as he realized I did not know the answers to his questions.

'You can't do this to us, Tara...' he said, growing teary-eyed. *I can't do this*, I thought to myself. I can't let him go. He's the best thing that has ever happened to me.

'There's another thing I need to tell you,' I said taking his hands in mine. 'I've liked you for a long time now. I don't know if you feel the same. Hell, I don't even know if you've ever noticed. The one thing I do know is that no matter how far apart we are and no matter how much time passes by, I will always care for you. I don—'

'Stop. Shut up for a second,' he said staring right into my eyes. 'I feel the same for you. I always have. It was so obvious. I don't even know how you never realized. I forget about the rest of the world when you're with me; everything seems so bleak compared to you. I know it's absurd to hear this given we're so young, but please, Tara, don't leave me.'

'I'm sorry, Jo. If I could prevent this from happening, I would. I wanted to tell you earlier, but I thought it would just make us spend my last days here worrying about the day I would finally have to leave.'

'What is happening here?' a voice said from behind me. I immediately let go of Jo's hands and turned around. It was Aliya and Rahul. Aliya gave me a look. She had always disapproved of the idea of me and Jo being together.

'She's moving,' Jo said.

'What? Is this true, Tara?' Aliya asked. Rahul just stared at my face dumbfounded as if he had just seen a ghost.

'Yes. I'm sorry I didn't tell you guys before. Today is my last day at school.'

'Tara, you can't do this. You can't just suddenly tell us such a thing thirty minutes before school starts,' Rahul said with tears starting to build in his eyes. He then proceeded to hug me and sob uncontrollably. I felt like a villain for the first time in my life. Finally, when Rahul stopped sobbing, Aliya and Jo burst into tears. It was like a contagious disease.

Seeing them cry made Rahul and me cry too. It was like a huge sob fest in Jo's backyard. Once things settled down, Jo went to get ready for school while I talked to Aliya and Rahul a bit more about where I was moving to. We then left for school, and after a couple of

WHAT A BEAUTIFUL ROSE!

hours, it was time for me to leave. I hugged my friends goodbye and embarked on a very sad start to a new and unnerving journey. I remember it was incredibly difficult to adjust at first, but eventually, I got along just fine.

∽

A couple of years passed. I made new friends. Sadly, I lost contact with my old ones. It was around the time I had just turned twenty-one. I was really happy at that point in life. I had amazing friends and an amazing boyfriend, and my relationship with my parents had improved immensely.

It was one of those nights when I was working late and had a lot of work. It was pouring outside with ear-shattering sounds of thunder tearing through the sky. I was leaving the building I worked in when I suddenly felt as if someone was watching me. I had reached the lobby when I felt a piercing gaze on me. I turned around only to see Jo standing with gorgeous yellow roses in his hand.

'Jo! Oh my god, it's been so long. It's so nice to see you. How have you been? What are you doing here?'

'Tara, there's something you need to know,' he paused for a second, 'I know her secret. I...I've got to go.'

'What? What are you talking about? At least tell me before going.'

'I'm sorry, Tara,' he said softly as he disappeared into the night taking the flowers with him.

Seeing Jo reminded me of Aliya and Rahul. I tried to find them on Facebook but could only get hold of Aliya. Neither Jo nor Rahul was to be found on any of those platforms. I talked to Aliya so I could fly out to meet her, visit my childhood home and hopefully find out more about what Jo had to say and where he was.

My boyfriend insisted on tagging along saying he didn't trust these people. He was creeped out by the fact that Jo suddenly appeared out of nowhere one day. I assured him that I had been with these people my whole childhood and that it was safe. He still wasn't convinced, and I decided to let him come with me.

The next morning, we left early for the airport. We reached in no time and stopped at my childhood home first.

It brought back lots of memories—good and bad. I knew Aliya had already moved, but I was curious to know if Jo and Rahul still lived here. I went over to Rahul's house, but it was bolted shut and looked like no one had lived there in years.

I went over to Jo's house next only to discover

another family was living there now. Soon after drowning in all the nostalgia, I left with my boyfriend for the cafe where we were supposed to meet Aliya. We sat in the cafe for about thirty minutes before Aliya reached. As she entered through the door, I was astonished by her beauty.

'Oh my god, Aliya. It's been ages! You look amazing.'

'Tara! Finally. I've missed you so much. You look great as well.'

A mere five seconds later, a tall buff man entered through the same door.

'Uh Tara, you remember Rahul.'

'Rahul? Jesus, you've changed so much. I barely recognized you. What a surprise!' I said as I went in for a hug.

'I've missed you so much, Tara,' he said getting teary-eyed. Maybe his physical appearance had changed, but he was still the same old emotional Rahul.

'Guys, I would like you to meet my boyfriend,' I said introducing them.

'Tara, we actually had another surprise for you,' Aliya said stretching her right hand towards me. 'Me and Rahul are engaged!'

'Oh. My. God. You've got to be kidding me! Congratulations, you guys. How did this happen?'

FANTASY, REALITY OR DELUSION?

'Oh, it's a long story. You must come to the wedding, no ifs or buts,' Rahul said, pulling up a chair.

We talked for over an hour, revisiting old memories that had been lost somewhere in my head. Somewhere along our conversation, Aliya mentioned Jo, which reminded me of our strange meeting.

'Oh, Aliya, do you know where Jo is now? I was hoping to talk to him about something.'

'Tara... Don't you know?' she said with a sudden shudder in her voice.

'What do I not know?'

'Jo died five years ago.'

'Wha-what? That cannot be possible,' I said, shocked. I froze, my mind froze. A chill ran down my spine, and goosebumps spread all over my body. Had I seen a ghost?

'I know it's a lot to take in. It was a most unfortunate incident. The police ruled his death a suicide, but we didn't believe it at all. We think he was murdered. We couldn't get the police to investigate further, and we couldn't gather enough evidence on our own.'

'That cannot be possible. I saw Jo just a few days ago. He was in the lobby of the building I work in with flowers in his hands. He said he had to tell me something, but then he apologized and left without saying anything more.'

'Tara, I think you're just in shock. We attended his funeral. He is gone however much we hate to admit it.'

I was in complete shock. I couldn't believe it. If Jo was really dead, who had I seen or, more importantly, what had I seen?

'We thought you met Jo just a little while before his death.'

'No, I hadn't seen him since the day I left town.'

'That's weird. I remember him mentioning that he had a chat with your father when he came to complete the sale of your old house. Jo also said he sent you an email, but perhaps, you never received it.'

'My father? He's never mentioned it. He never even told me he came back here. That's weird. Maybe he sent it to my old email; I don't use it any more. I'll try logging in.'

'Oh, perhaps you should ask your father about it when you go back.'

'Do you guys have any more details about his death?'

'He died of a bullet to his head. His body was discovered on the morning of the 1st of July in the middle of the very street we lived on. People say no one heard a gunshot, but it was pretty evident he died of a gunshot. The weapon was never recovered, but we believe the killer still has it. It was a pretty common pistol, so

FANTASY, REALITY OR DELUSION?

you'd imagine it'd be hard to identify,' said Aliya.

'Even his parents pushed for an investigation, but you know how the police are in small towns. They ruled it a suicide because of a lack of evidence. I don't understand how the gun wouldn't still be there if it was a suicide. Nevertheless, at that point, we hadn't seen him for weeks. It was most heartbreaking. We couldn't bear the loss and moved away,' Rahul said taking Aliya's hand in his.

Soon enough, it was time to go back home. The whole time on the aeroplane I kept thinking about what I had seen and why my father never told me about this interaction. I didn't want to discuss what I had seen any further; I was scared people would think I had lost my mind or gone crazy. Even my boyfriend had started doubting my sanity. I reached home and straight away went to my father's room.

'Hello, Dad.'

'Oh, hi sweetheart. How was your trip?'

'Fine. You haven't seen Jo anytime recently, have you?'

'You come back after days and that's the first thing you ask me? Sweetheart, he died years ago. I thought you knew.'

'Quit avoiding my question. Did you see Jo before he died?'

'No, sweetheart. How and where would I see him?'

'You're lying to me. I know you saw him before he died. I know you went back to complete the sale of our old house, and he came to you.'

'Tara, I swear I don't know what you're talking about.'

'Fine, keep lying to me. I'll just go to my room.'

I entered my room barely holding back my tears. My old best friend was dead, and my dad was lying to me about seeing him. What could I possibly do? I sat on my bed as I tried to access my old email.

I tried and tried but couldn't remember the password. Eventually, I gave up. I texted a colleague to help me the next day. Later, I lay down on my bed with a million thoughts running through my head. I couldn't sleep a wink. This feeling was intensely familiar and just as annoying.

The next morning, as I headed to work, I handed the login credentials of my old email to my co-worker and went about completing my tasks for the day. However, I couldn't focus. I kept trying to distract myself, but the possibility of Jo being murdered kept disturbing me.

Soon enough, my co-worker called me to say he had been successful in recovering my old email. I ran over to his desk as fast as I could. I took his laptop into a separate room for a while. I saw the email he had sent.

FANTASY, REALITY OR DELUSION?

It was an audio file. The quality was horrendous, but I could make out his voice.

'Sir, can you calm down? If Tara finds out about you saying all of this, she wouldn't like it.'

Suddenly, a very familiar voice replied. A shudder went down my spine. I couldn't believe it. It was my father.

'My daughter would never marry the likes of you. Your father has ruined me. I would never allow it to happen.'

'S-Sir, you're drunk. Please can you put the gun down?' Jo said in a terrified voice.

'You're lucky I was gifted this gun today, so it's not loaded. Come anywhere near my family again and I will kill you.'

The recording ended. I couldn't believe my ears. A feeling of dread took over me. Was it possible my dad killed Jo?

I rushed home and saw my dad on the balcony smoking a cigar. I ran up to him sobbing uncontrollably.

'DAD, WHAT HAVE YOU DONE?' I screamed at the top of my lungs.

'Sweetie, what happened? Why are you crying? Is everything okay?'

'Give me the keys to your locker. NOW!' I screamed. It was where he stored his gun, which was apparently a 'gift'.

'Okay, okay. Calm down,' he said as he handed me the keys.

'Not this one, the big one.'

'Sweetie, you know I don't let anyone look at that locker.'

'I SAID NOW!' I screamed my lungs out.

He handed me the keys. As I opened the locker, I saw a sight I couldn't believe. It was a bunch of jewellery and cash along with huge packets of white powder, which I assumed to be drugs.

Worst of all, a pistol lay in the middle.

I panicked. My heartbeat increased. I ran outside as fast as I could. My father tried to approach me, but I screamed, 'STAY THE HELL AWAY FROM ME!'

I got into my car and drove as fast as I could to the nearest police station. I told them everything. I couldn't believe it at first, but everything added up. He killed Jo out of hatred towards his father. I was devastated. I gave the police all the proof I had. His gun matched the murder weapon. He was arrested immediately.

He kept telling me how Mr Ramson gifted him the gun and it was for his safety, but all I heard were excuses. I was miserable for a few weeks. My mother couldn't believe it. She was depressed, and it disheartened me to see her that way. All our income was cut off, and I was

FANTASY, REALITY OR DELUSION?

the sole provider now. My father kept denying killing him, but the evidence proved otherwise. It was the most traumatizing month of my life.

Not long after all this happened, I went to visit Jo's sister. She told me something unusual about the night he died.

'Before he died, he kept telling me, "I know her secret. She mustn't find out I know, sister. Her secret could land her in jail. I don't know what to do." He never told me who "she" was or what the secret was.' That was the same thing he had said to me the night I saw him, but I convinced myself I was thinking too much and brushed it off.

The next month, I flew back to my home town for Aliya and Rahul's wedding. I was so happy after so long. Seeing my childhood friends get married filled my heart with joy. I saw Mr Ramson, who was Aliya's father. He seemed really happy.

At the wedding, I made a crucial observation that made my heart sink for a moment as the whole picture suddenly became clearer to me.

The flowers were yellow roses—Aliya's favourite—which I had completely forgotten. They were the same flowers that Jo was carrying the day I saw him.

WHAT A BEAUTIFUL ROSE!

She owned a gun manufacturing company, and Jo kept referring to 'her secret'.

Also, on the day I met Aliya, she mentioned Jo telling her about the email and also that she hadn't seen him in weeks, but the recording was emailed to me barely hours before his death.

How could Aliya possibly know about that? As I came to this realization, I looked at her, and her face suddenly seemed different.

Was I thinking too much or did I send the wrong person to jail? I was in over my head and didn't know what I was doing. Aliya noticed me looking off and came over to me.

'You know, you'll never be able to prove it was me,' she said with a wide grin on her face. My smile suddenly dropped as horror gripped me and made me shudder with fear.

'He knew too much. Sadly, it had to end that way. I did care for him, but he only cared for you. He knew what I'd sacrificed to expand my father's company. If he told the police that I was a murderer, it would all go to waste. How does it feel knowing you're not only the reason Jo's dead but also why your dad's in jail? Utter a word and I will end you and the little family you have left. Now, smile, Tara. Enjoy the rest of the party,' she said as my teary-eyed face suddenly lit up despite guilt consuming my heart.

I put on a façade, a burden I carried my whole life. I spent a long time trying to figure out how to make amends.

Looks are deceptive. The truth is always much more complicated.

9

I WAS ALL OVER HER

'Good morning, smally.' I yawned as I woke up. My cat was sleeping beside me, cuddled up on the pillow next to mine.

It was a lousy Sunday morning, sometime around eleven. I barely had the energy to drag myself out of bed and go make breakfast. I gasped as I opened the curtains to my balcony; it was raining.

I have a love–hate relationship with rain. Rain makes the world a different place, and its feeling is just unmatchable. It is so beautiful yet brings about such gloom and sadness.

At the same time, rain is really annoying and ruins all plans.

FANTASY, REALITY OR DELUSION?

I took my phone off the charger and held down the power button so that I could turn it on. As my phone's screen slowly came to life, I placed it on the kitchen counter and opened the fridge. I stared at it for about thirty seconds before deciding I wanted to have eggs.

As I took the eggs out of the fridge, my phone automatically connected with the Wi-Fi and notifications started popping up. There were like a million notifications. This was surprising considering I barely talk to people over text. I have ten to fifteen friends, and I am not in contact with some of them for weeks.

It's not necessarily because I don't like them or I don't enjoy their company. It's just that I get annoyed really quickly. Some people don't know the meaning of friendship and invade others' personal space. These stupid people instigate fights just for drama and entertainment.

No matter how much I love fighting when I'm right, I have neither the time nor the patience to deal with or argue with seventy people each and every day. I'm not implying having a huge friend circle is necessarily a bad thing, but it does attract a lot of drama and problems.

Anyway, my curiosity rose as I sat on my kitchen counter to go through the enormous number of notifications I had received.

I WAS ALL OVER HER

As I scrolled through my notifications, I noticed more than thirty texts from my best friend. *What the hell happened?*

'WHAT HAVE YOU DONE?'

'ARE YOU SERIOUSLY STILL SLEEPING?'

'WAKE UP RIGHT NOW! WHAT IS WRONG WITH YOU?'

'DO YOU KNOW HOW MUCH TROUBLE YOU'RE IN?'

'I'M ASHAMED TO CALL YOU MY BEST FRIEND.'

These were some of the texts I had gotten from her. What was she talking about? I immediately called her up. The phone rang a few times before she picked up the call and instantly started screaming at me.

'Have you gone insane? What were you thinking? Do you know how much trouble you could be in right now? Are you using again?'

'What are you talking about? Have you lost it? I haven't done shit.'

'What do you mean you haven't done shit? Now you're not even going to admit it? Even a ten-year-old knows how to hold themselves accountable for their actions.'

'Bro, I seriously don't know what you're talking about. Unless you're going to explain what has happened, I will never know.'

'You showed no regret after a woman accused you of making her uncomfortable. Are you going to deny that now?'

'What the hell are you talking about? Do you really think I would do something like that? Who in their right mind would spread such a rumour?'

'Rumour? I have proof. VIDEO PROOF! Also, I thought you were sleeping in last night. I told you not to go to that shady party. Well, turns out you're the shady guy, not them.'

'What party are you talking about? I was watching Netflix all night yesterday; I didn't step out of my house for even a second. I ordered from Taco Bell and ate like a cow. If you want, you can see my order history. And what video? How can there possibly be a video when I wasn't even there? You know I'm not that kind of guy. I would never harm a woman.'

'Okay, well, explain this then. Check your texts.'

What followed was one of the most horrific and astonishing things I've ever seen in my life.

When I checked my phone, I had been sent a video. It was about a minute long. I played it. It started off shaky, and I couldn't see anything, but about five seconds in, I could see a girl screaming with tears running down her face.

In front of her was a figure about three or four inches taller than her. He was standing with his back towards the camera, and I couldn't fully see his face. His hair was kind of like mine. The girl slapped him, and as he held his face, I could see what he looked like from one angle.

He looked exactly like me. I gasped.

He showed no remorse, and as the girl kept slapping him, a smirk stayed plastered across his face. Who was he? The girl kept accusing him of heinous acts, but the smile remained stagnant. Not too long after, he stepped out of the frame and—I assume—out of the door without a word.

I was awestruck. I did not know what to say.

'That is not me. Trust me, I will prove it to you,' I said as I cut the call to think for a while. What had I just witnessed? Was that even physically or scientifically possible?

Just as I had started to clear my head and think, my phone started ringing again. This time, it was my sister.

'You owe me one for last night. Don't do stupid stuff like that ever again. You're a grown-up now. Do you really expect me to clean up your mess at this age?'

'What do you mean? What did I do?' I said confused.

FANTASY, REALITY OR DELUSION?

'Don't you remember? Were you that drunk? You got caught drunk driving. You're lucky I have friends at the police station; otherwise, you'd still be in jail. You should enjoy your life as you please, but don't do stuff that can get you or someone else killed. Stay careful next time. See you soon. Love you,' she said as she hung up. There was a blank look on my face.

What? I immediately ran over to my window to see if my car was still there. It wasn't. Who was this man, and what was he doing with my life?

My first thought was to go to the police, which did not sound like a good idea considering I had just gotten arrested the night before, that too for drinking too much. It wasn't actually me of course, but the police would think I'd lost it.

So I booked a taxi instead and went to the place where the party was. I rang the guy's doorbell, and after a few explanations and efforts to assure him I meant no harm, I managed to get the name of the girl who had gone home with me or rather him.

I called her and asked about the guy. She said, and I quote, 'He was really weird. As soon as we reached his home, he panicked and asked me to leave. But why should I give you any information?'

After a while of acting like the good guy and giving

her some money through an app, I managed to get some more information.

'His house is on Roseberry Cliff, just next to where the stairs to the beach start.'

This man was really affecting my reputation. Who was he, and why was he doing this? I had never gotten into a scandal before, and I highly valued my loved ones' opinions. I might just go crazy at this point. I thought about going to his place a million times over in my head. Was it safe? I had to do something; I couldn't just sit idle.

I told the taxi driver to drop me off on the far side of Roseberry Cliff, not wanting to alert my lookalike. I walked the rest of the way till I saw a house just at the edge of the cliff. A man stood outside smoking what looked like a cigar.

'So, you're the one ruining my life?' I asked walking up to him and standing right beside him.

He turned around. He looked just like me. It was unnaturally freaky. How can this man look exactly like me and not be biologically related to me? Was it real? Or was I seeing things?

'Oh my friend, our resemblance is uncanny. Wow. I'm not planning to stop any time soon. I have other plans in mind.'

'Really? And what if I report you?'

'Well, you won't be able to. The police will just think you're drunk again. Even if the police somehow manage to find us together, enough destruction will have been caused by then.'

'What do you mean? What have you done this time?'

'Would you like to see?' he said as he pulled out a human finger with a ring on it. It wasn't just any ring; it was my mom's engagement ring. I was shocked. My face displayed the horror I was experiencing in my heart.

'Oh, this is nothing. There's a bomb in her house set to explode in about two minutes. She's tied up. She can't escape, and the bomb cannot be disabled. I have ruined you.'

'What? Why are you doing this? What will you get out of this?'

My ears couldn't believe what they were hearing. My heart filled with anger and sorrow. I couldn't take it, not any more. I had to stop this. Without a second thought, I grabbed him by the collar and threw him off the cliff.

But instead of seeing him fall, I felt myself falling. WHAT? As I fell, I saw him standing atop the same cliff. He blew smoke from his cigar and screamed, 'I'm not human, you fool. I can't die.'

In various myths, it is said that a doppelgänger is

FANTASY, REALITY OR DELUSION?

essentially the ghost of a living person. Seeing your doppelgänger in real life brings bad luck or even death.

If you see someone with the same face as yours, run and do not look back.

10

PARADISE

When I was young, I read many books about kids' adventures in a fantasy world. All my favourite authors never disappointed me while writing stories with such exquisite detail that it was hard not to believe they were real. I would crave having the same adventures and meeting all of the fantastical creatures that existed.

I never used to get dreams until one day, I went to sleep and awoke in a forest. It was a weirdly bright forest. Everything seemed much more alive than in the real world.

To make sure I was dreaming, I pinched myself, but it actually hurt. Confused and scared, I wondered how

I'd gotten there.

'Are you looking for something, young lady?' a squeaky voice screeched from behind me. It startled me a little. I turned around only to find a human, but short, a dwarf, if you may.

He was wearing a most peculiar hat; it was a mix of all colours. I stared at him for a while, forgetting it is rude to stare before he said something.

'Ahem, miss, exactly how long are you planning to stand here and gawk at me?'

'Oh! I'm so sorry. I did not mean to stare. Would you be so kind as to tell me where I am? I've never seen this place before, and I am kind of confused as to how I got here.'

'You're in a place called Mirabili. If you're new here, I could show you around if you wish.'

I was more astonished than confused at this point. The dwarf spoke in an accent I had never heard, and his voice was so funny and squeaky that I was barely able to hold myself back from cracking up.

'Yes, that would be wonderful. Thank you, dear ... I'm sorry, I didn't catch your name,' I said.

'Resmin, dear child. You can call me Resmin. Now, off we go. An adventure awaits!'

As we walked deeper into the woods, the scenery

around us kept turning more and more colourful. Gorgeous wildflowers were growing beneath humongous trees with exotic birds moving through them. It was a most enchanting sight.

'Where are we going, sir, if I may ask?'

'We are going to a place so fantastical you will never forget it. This is Mirabili, my dear. Nothing disappoints.'

On our way to our destination, we crossed a lake where I could see a magical-looking deer with magnificent antlers drinking water. It was beautiful.

Soon, we reached our destination. It was the most stunning, extraordinary and mystical sight I had ever seen. We were standing at the edge of a huge waterfall, and I could see an amazing number of species of vegetation and wildlife extending as far as one could see.

The sun was just setting, and I could see numerous birds flying across the sky. The scene seemed like it was out of a fantasy book. I slowly exhaled, taking in all the beauty I could see before me.

'This is Point Mira. From here, you can probably see all of Mirabili. It is one of the most beautiful wonders of our world.'

'I...I have no words. This is exceptional. It seems like I'm living in a fairy tale.'

PARADISE

'It is a fairy tale, child, and I'm afraid it's time for you to go back.'

'Whatever do you me—' Before I could complete my sentence, I woke up with a jolt.

Wow, that felt so real. I can't believe it was all a dream. That scenery will remain forever etched in my mind.

My childhood was complete. I hope I'm able to revisit Mirabili, even if it's in my dreams.

That place reminds me of one word, and one word only: **Paradise.**

11

OH, DEAR JAMIE

Oh, dear Jamie,
What a lovely girl.
Smart as a bookworm,
With a face as beautiful as a pearl.
She lives on the corner,
The corner of Westbrook Lane.
Selling books for a living,
Devoid of any pain

Oh, dear Jamie,
What a lovely dress she wears,
Flowers scattered all over her skirt,
As soft as silk is her hair.

FANTASY, REALITY OR DELUSION?

She hops around the market,
Buying her daily goods,
Never bargaining,
Or taking advantage of her looks.

Oh, dear Jamie,
What a sharp brain she possesses!
Failing even the smartest of them all,
Making insignificant their successes.
The youngsters leave,
Leave while feeling dysphoric.
Even while this sweet victory,
Never seems to make her euphoric.

Oh, dear Jamie,
How society failed.
Failed to protect you from yourself,
All the while you wailed.
No one heard your cries for help,
However silent they might have been.
How could we have known you're a sociopath?
When you were just a really lovely teen.

12

XOXO, THE ANTIQUE BURGLAR

Not so long ago, in an irrelevant town, lived a man. He hated his life, much like the other seven billion people on this planet.

He looked down at the bustle in the street with a cigarette in his hand, blowing away the stress he hadn't experienced yet but was soon going to, being surrounded by the idiots he called co-workers. Venkat Bakshi, his badge said. Venkat worked at the Sadar Bazar Police Station, mostly against his will.

FANTASY, REALITY OR DELUSION?

My mom worked in the police force, so I felt compelled to do the same. Even if I didn't feel like it, my parents made sure I did. I wanted to be a researcher. My passion is chemistry, but my parents felt otherwise. Against their will, I opened a makeshift lab in my house in a room that they wanted me to turn into a home gym.

I'm dealing with this torture only so that I can save enough to follow my dreams without having to worry about money.

I walked down the hallway to my office, dreading the day I had ahead of me.

'Wow, Venkat, the audacity you have to walk into this office after butchering a case is insane,' one of my colleagues, Ritesh said, laughing. This comment made the room erupt in laughter.

Ritesh has had a personal agenda against me since the day I joined the force. He believes I'm privileged to have a mom who worked in the force, unlike his parents who wanted him to become an engineer. He gives me a hard time about it, as do my other colleagues, but at this point, these comments have made their way into my everyday life.

'He should've become a chemist only. It suits him well. At least the citizens would not have to worry about not getting justice,' Devraj, a colleague and Ritesh's best friend, said.

My blood boiled when I heard such words come out of his mouth, but over the years, I had learned it was best not to react. I ignored their stupid comments, '*Ek kaan se suno, ek kaan se nikalo,*' my mother had taught me. 'Listen through one ear and let it out through the other.'

I sat down at my desk, contemplating about the case I had messed up the previous day. 'What are you thinking about, Venky?' a voice called out from behind me. It was my only friend in the precinct, Prabhat.

'If it's about what those fools keep saying, it is because they're jealous of you. They wait for you to mess up so that they can point it out and feel better about themselves. Just ignore them.'

'I know, Prabhat, but sometimes I wonder how different my life would've been if I had followed my dreams.'

'Chal, let it go. Tell me, are you free tonight? Me, Sara, Rohit and Mira are going to the new club that has opened on 22nd Street. Rohit said he'll get us in as he and the owner have some mutual friends.'

'Well, I'm in the middle of conducting an experiment on cobalt compounds. It's actually very interesting. You know, right now, I'm—'

'Enough, enough,' Prabhat cut me off. 'Stop being a nerd and live a little, man. Continue your experiment tomorrow. Tonight, you're coming to party with us.'

Even though the idea of abandoning my experiment bothered me a little, I agreed to join them.

The day passed like any other.

As I was leaving for the night, I heard Devraj say, 'What a weirdo this Venkat is. He has close to no life. He has no love life and almost no real friends. Hell, the only thing he has is his chemicals. I wonder how he survives such loneliness.'

Even though my heart wished to punch him right in the gut at that moment, I resisted the urge to do so. *What a lifeless brat. How pathetic a life you must have to say such stuff about another human being*, I thought to myself.

As I got into my car, I noticed a letter attached to my windshield. It was plain white, with a mark of a kiss made by someone wearing purple lipstick. Weird. I took it out of my windshield and threw it on the back seat of my car. It was a windy day, and I'm the kind of person who feels chilly even in the scorching heat of May. As I made my way home, I could faintly make out the silhouette of the moon—so quiet, so peaceful, so precious and elegant.

It was already late when I reached home, so I quickly changed into fresh clothes and set out for the club.

As I approached the club, I could see a tall buff guy

standing at the entrance, staring me up and down like I was a piece of meat.

'Hey, Venkat, over here!' Rohit called out. I could see him waving his hand from a distance. I began to make my way inside and was stopped by the buff guy. 'Where do you think you're going?' he said. 'I...I...I'm...My friends—' I stuttered. By then, Rohit had come over and said, 'He's with me,' to which the buff guy reacted as if I was his childhood friend and welcomed me gracefully.

'Tell me one thing, Venkat,' Sara said as I neared the table, 'how is it you're a police officer but still fear a bouncer who is basically incapable of hurting you in any way?'

I giggled. 'What can I say, Sara? Tall buff guys scare me. Anyway, guys, I hope I didn't make you wait too long,' I said.

'No, not long at all, just about one and a half hours,' Mira laughed, looking quite beautiful I must say.

I was just getting comfortable and swaying to the music when I got a call. I made my way into the men's room and answered my phone. It was the captain.

'Sorry to disturb you in your free time, Venkat, but there has been a burglary just off 22nd Street. Prabhat told me you guys were going to a club nearby. I'm going to need you both to head over to the scene.'

FANTASY, REALITY OR DELUSION?

Oh lovely, even the universe hates it when I socialize. Guess I'm meant to be lonely forever.

I informed Prabhat and we headed over to the scene.

By the time we arrived, a lot of officers were already there consoling a teenage girl. I made my way over to her.

'Hello, what might be your name?'

'Sheila. My name's Sheila.'

'How old are you, Sheila? Do you work here?'

'I'm seventeen. I don't work here, but I sometimes look after the shop when my grandfather's out.'

'Could you tell me what happened? Don't spare any details.'

'I...I was talking to a friend on the phone when I heard the bell on the front door ring. I wasn't paying much attention, so I didn't see who had walked in. I continued talking to my friend until I heard something shatter behind me. It was a vase. I cut the call and went over to the aisle to see what had happened, but I saw no one. Just as I made my way towards the front to see who it was, I heard the bell ring again and the sound of someone walking quickly making 'tik, tik, tik' sounds. I didn't see who it was and found the whole thing weird. As I headed back to the counter, I saw that one of the showpieces was gone. It was a gem my grandfather had brought back from his trip to Egypt and wasn't on sale. He just liked to show off his most prized possession. It was kept in a safe, which sounded an alarm any time someone touched it, but the safe had been busted open. My grandfather will be so mad at me.'

'Okay, Sheila, thank you. Please don't fret because it's not your fault. Is that all? Could you tell us the estimated price of the gem and describe it for us? Or perhaps you have a picture?'

'It has been valued at ₹5–8 crore, but we have also gotten offers of ₹15–20 crore. I'll show you its picture that I have on my phone.'

What the hell! ₹20 crore, are you kidding me? ₹20 crore would literally solve all my life problems twenty times over! That's insane, and what's crazier is to leave such possession under the supervision of a teenager. Good heavens! I thought to myself as she took out her phone to show me the picture.

The gem was dark orange in colour and oval in shape. It was placed on top of a metal plate within a glass display case.

'Thank you, Sheila. You've helped our investigation immensely,' I said and started walking away from her.

I made my way over to Prabhat, and we started walking towards the car.

FANTASY, REALITY OR DELUSION?

'So, did you enjoy meeting my friends, Venky?' he asked.

'They're nice, but Prabhat, you do know your friends are a little over the top. They're major alcoholics and some even do drugs regularly. I heard Mira was in rehab for drug addiction, Sara for alcoholism and Rohit almost got caught trying to sell multiple types of drugs!'

'I mean, Rohit is the reason Mira was in rehab. He sold coke to her when she was at her most vulnerable, and look where she's ended up. Sara's family's a bit cuckoo, which resulted in her becoming dependent on alcohol, but they eventually realized what they were doing when she almost died. I know they went through a bad phase, but they're not bad people. They're trying to improve day by day.'

Even though Prabhat reassured me his friends were safe to trust, I was not keen on interacting with them again.

I sat in my car and made my way home. It was so late at night that I felt like melting into my bed. I was getting out of the car when I noticed the letter in the back seat. I grabbed it and went inside.

I took a shower and changed into my nightwear. I was highly disappointed that I wouldn't be able to work on my ongoing experiment. I drank some milk and was

XOXO, THE ANTIQUE BURGLAR

about to retire for the night when I saw the letter on my drawing room table. What could it be?

I flipped it around. The letter was sealed with a wax stamp that had the image of a stallion on it. I ripped open the envelope, inside which was a yellow colour card—the same kind you buy for birthdays or anniversaries.

As I opened the card, the sweet sound of music filled the drawing room. It was Kishore Kumar's 'Inteha Ho Gayi Intezaar Ki' (it's been a long wait). Inside the card were some flowers and a typed message that said 'Best of Luck for All Your Future Endeavours!' Just below that was a printed message, which was evidently stuck on by the same person who sent it.

> At last we meet, Venkat Bakshi. I've heard quite a lot about you. If you're as smart as I think you are, you won't have much trouble figuring out who I am. And if you're as smart as you think you are, you'll have no problem arresting me for the burglary. Safe to say, I will stay one step ahead of you. Catch me if you can. I'll be watching you.
> Xoxo, The Antique Burglar

'How...' I said to myself. I looked around to see if my windows were shut. I had been feeling sleepy, but this

FANTASY, REALITY OR DELUSION?

woke me up. I scurried around for a while trying to process what I had just read. It was the same person who had robbed the antique store.

But some things threw me off.

First, there was a lipstick stain on the front of the envelope.

Second, Sheila had mentioned 'tik, tik, tik' sounds, which would imply the person was wearing heels.

Third, the culprit had used 'Xoxo' at the end of their letter.

All these things pointed to the obvious: the culprit was a lady. Or was the culprit depending on the fact that I would conclude it's a lady by pointing out the obvious?

Fourth, the culprit had challenged my abilities as well as told me they were 'watching me'. What did that mean?

The fifth thing was that the culprit must have known I was going to be somewhere nearby because the letter was kept on my windshield well before I had reached my destination. A million other inspectors could have been assigned this case, but they knew it was going to come to me.

The only promising lead I could think of was checking the station cameras to see if they caught who had delivered the letter.

XOXO, THE ANTIQUE BURGLAR

I let out a large yawn and rubbed my eyes. It was too late, and my brain was tired, so I delayed the investigation till the next morning.

I woke up the next morning when a beam of sunshine pierced my curtains. I got up and became ready for work as fast as I could. As I walked down the hallway, Ritesh felt the need to pass an unnecessary comment. 'The old man that runs the antique shop has run out of luck it seems. He got the worst inspector assigned to his case,' he said, chuckling like he had cracked the world's greatest joke. I ignored it and went straight to the captain.

'Good morning, Venkat. Any updates on the case?' he enquired as his gaze went towards the letter in my hand.

'Sir, I don't know how but I think the burglar is targeting me,' I said as I extended my hand to give him the letter.

His eyes grew wide as he opened the letter and then the card. The sweet melody of the song filled his office. He then proceeded to think for a moment with his hand on his head.

'How did you get this letter? And what's with the weird song?' he asked finally, breaking the silence.

'It was left on the windshield of my car, sir, when I

was here. At first, I paid no heed to it, but last night, after I reached home, I opened the letter and found this. I need to check the security cameras to see who kept the letter on my car.'

'Okay, Venkat, you do that. Call me as soon as you get an update. And be safe. This burglar could be nursing a grudge against you.'

I quietly shuffled out of the office, shutting the door behind me. As I made my way to the security room, I wondered who would do such a thing just to challenge me. No immediate names came to mind.

What a bore! I thought to myself. I would have to sit through around six to seven hours of footage.

I retrieved the footage from the security room and sat down in one of the interrogation rooms to watch it. I was about two hours in when I noticed a man walking towards my car. He was wearing a uniform, a yellow shirt with green sleeves and a logo on the front.

Greenrow Enterprise.

Greenrow Enterprise was the largest courier service in the city. The hassle of locating a single employee would take up my whole day.

Disappointed, I made my way to their headquarters. It was a thirty-minute drive. Soon enough, I reached their office and was greeted by a man named Ramesh.

He told me his last name as well, but it was so long I couldn't memorize it.

I remember thinking, 'What a peculiar man.' He was wearing clothes that didn't match at all. Who wears a yellow striped tie with a pink polka dot shirt!?! His gait was weird too. He had a kind of limp, which I noticed when he got up and walked around his table towards me.

'What do you need, Inspector?' he asked.

'Good morning. An employee from your company delivered a letter to me. I was wondering if you could help identify him,' I said and proceeded to show him a picture.

'I'm sorry, sir, but I've never seen that man before. If you go up to the sixth floor, you'll find the HR department. Someone will be able to help you there.'

I thanked the man and made my way upstairs. I got into the lift. Standing next to me was a woman dressed in a suit and wearing high heels. She had auburn hair and green eyes. Her perfume was so strong it made me sneeze. I assumed she was going to the tenth floor because it was the only other button pressed other than the sixth.

'Excuse me,' I said while covering my face with my hands. She offered me a tissue.

'Thank you, miss,' I said accepting it.

FANTASY, REALITY OR DELUSION?

I reached the sixth floor and bid the woman goodbye.

The sixth floor contained what you could only call a nest of cubicles. There was so much chaos; everyone was engrossed in their work. Somehow, I caught the attention of a young boy and asked him where the hiring manager was. He showed me to his office.

The hiring manager was a handsome man, even if on the shorter side. He wore a blue coloured suit with a beautiful tie. His hair was slicked back, and one of his ears was pierced.

'Inspector! How can I help you?' he said, acting a little astonished, but I mean, anyone would get startled if an inspector showed up at their office out of nowhere.

I showed the man the picture, and his face lit up.

'This is Sunil. We hired him just over a week ago. His résumé was incredible. I really don't know why he decided to take it. Anyway, he sent in his resignation this morning. How strange! He barely lasted a week. Is he in some kind of trouble?'

'No, sir. No trouble. If it's not a problem, could you give me his contact information or an address?'

'Sure, Inspector. I'll have the receptionist print it out for you, so you can collect it from the front desk.'

In my car, as I read through the printout, I realized the man lived suspiciously close to the antique shop.

XOXO, THE ANTIQUE BURGLAR

I made my way to his house. Could he be the thief? Would it be that easy to catch the burglar?

The neighbourhood he lived in was quite shabby. His house was located in an apartment complex on the eighth floor. The sign that read 'No. 31' on his door was crooked, and the door looked as if it was very old. A man opened the door. He was the one from the footage.

I pulled out my handcuffs, which may have startled the man a little, but unlike others, he did not make a dash for it. Instead, he said, 'Inspector, please, just hear me out. I have done no harm. I was told to put that letter on your window by an anonymous caller. They were the ones that asked me to apply for the job as well. I'm actually a method actor. They agreed to pay me ₹50,000 for this. I could not refuse, sir. I'm a poor man, as you can see. My career is not going very well. I'm sorry, I know nothing further. They also told me to give you a box.'

He started heading inside to grab the box, but I stopped him. I asked him where it was and retrieved it myself. Then, we proceeded towards the station to question him.

Prabhat interrogated the man while I tried opening the box. It was a resin box equipped with some type of latch mechanism that took me quite some time to figure out. When I finally pried it open, there was a rose attached to a higher platform inside the box and in front of it was a mirror.

The rose started rotating just as the box opened and played the same song as before, but it was a sped-up version. There was another smaller box inside the larger box, which contained an orange-coloured gem, but it did not require a professional to deduce that it was plastic. There was another note inside the box.

> Oh Venky, you underestimate me. You really didn't think it would be that easy, did you? I hope you're ready to chase after me if you want the gem back. Waiting for you.
> Xoxo, The Antique Burglar

The font type and size were the same as the last card, but something was different. This one had a scent to it. It was a very familiar scent, but for the life of me, I could not recognize what it was.

As I sat there contemplating where I'd smelled that scent before, I received a phone call.

And just like that, the Antique Burglar had struck again.

This time, it was another shop on 22nd Street called 'The World in One Room'.

'The World in One Room' was a shop famously known for its weird trinkets from all around the world. The fact that the Antique Burglar had chosen to rob a shop with nothing of extreme value was weirder. It was more a museum than a shop.

These thoughts ran through my mind as I made my way to 22nd Street. As I squeezed my car through the narrow lanes, I could already make out the chaos from a mile away.

The scene was flooded with passers-by as well as multiple officers trying to prevent them from coming inside the police tapes.

I ducked beneath the tape and noticed shards of glass from the shattered window scattered on the street, presumably because of the big rock lying on the ground. The rock also had a note tied to it. Before investigating the rock further, I went inside the shop to take a look. I saw two old men and a young girl standing near the counter.

'Hello, I'm Inspector Bakshi. I'm the chief inspector on this case. Could you please tell me what happened?' I asked.

'Inspector Bakshi, this is my brother and his daughter. The shop was closed when the robbery happened. The thief somehow got through our door without damaging it but could not get out without shattering one of our windows. Nothing important was stolen, just a little compass that one of our friends had gifted us. The compass is from Croatia and is said to have major historical significance. I reported the crime mainly because of damage to property. I was at my brother's when the alarm was triggered, so he agreed to drive me here.'

The man did not seem extremely disappointed with his loss, just as I thought. What was the Antique Burglar's motive?

I was taking down notes based on my surroundings when the young girl came up to me with a membership card in her hand.

'What is this, sweetie? Where did you find it?' I asked her.

She gestured towards the floor beside one of the shelves without saying a word. She then ran away towards her father.

By the time the investigation wound up, it was very late, so I left for home and decided to carry on the investigation the following day.

Despite having a long day and employing every possible method to get to sleep, for some reason, I was wide awake. So I decided to continue with my research for a little while. I put my gloves on and started working. After about an hour or so, I was tired and retired to bed without cleaning my set-up.

The next morning, I awoke early and made my way to the station. As you may have guessed, my lovely morning started with Ritesh's backhanded greetings, but this time, I actually couldn't care less. I had to figure out who the thief was. I made my way over to the evidence room.

I carefully took out the note from the sealed bag it was in and read it.

Venkat, honestly, you're too naïve for a detective. Did you think I would stop? Find me, Venkat. Find me before I raid every single shop in this town just for your attention. Best of luck; you'll need it.
Xoxo, The Antique Burglar

Who was this? Who would go to such an extent just to catch MY attention? It felt so wrong. I was lost in my thoughts when Prabhat came in.

'Oh, Venky, good I found you here. We're going over to 254 Cornelia Drive. I'll brief you on the way there,' he said.

In the car, Prabhat told me that the delivery guy had received a phone call from an unknown number. He was

FANTASY, REALITY OR DELUSION?

paid by mail three times, all of which came from the same address. The phone turned out to be a burner, but the address was real. That's where we are headed right now.

When we reached the address, the house in front of us was small but beautiful. It was pretty well kept.

We rang the doorbell and waited for around a minute, but there was no response. We were about to shout when we heard the sound of glass shattering. We kicked the door down at once and with guns in our hands started walking inside slowly. We quietly moved to the living room where we saw an old woman sitting on a recliner. At first, she did not notice us but was startled when she did. We tried to talk to her; when she realized we were trying to say something, she put on her hearing aids.

'What's wrong, Inspector?' she said, the words barely making it out of her mouth.

I looked at Prabhat in awe and mouthed, 'Her? Really?' before almost bursting out laughing.

She told us, 'I'm an old woman. I live alone. My nurse comes and visits me once a week. If someone has used my mailbox, I do not know and I do not care. I always love helping people out. That's it. I have committed no crime.'

XOXO, THE ANTIQUE BURGLAR

This was it. We had reached a dead end. We left the house with a frown on our faces. Now, the only piece of evidence left was the membership card.

As soon as we reached the police station, we started investigating the membership card.

It was for a book club called 'The Bookkeepers'. The forensics department tried lifting fingerprints off it but no luck. We tried calling the number for the club mentioned on the website but instead reached the shop it was usually held in.

They informed us that the club had been discontinued six years ago, and no records were kept of its members. That was it. Our last piece of evidence led to nothing. I returned home with a sad face and defeated spirits.

To further worsen my mood, one of my beakers fell and broke. The solution spilt all over the floor. When I tried to clean up the glass, I forgot that the solution was highly toxic and some of it got smeared on my hands.

I got up immediately and ran to the sink to wash my hands when I noticed they had turned blue. After washing my hands, I went back to see which container had broken, and suddenly, it all came into view.

The container that was broken was a cobalt compound called cobalt thiocyanate.

FANTASY, REALITY OR DELUSION?

It was one of the compounds I was studying and is famously used for Scott's test.

It is a colour-detecting test that turns blue when it reacts with cocaine.

The last thing I had touched before returning home was the membership card, which meant the burglar was a cocaine addict.

Suddenly everything fell into place. The scent had seemed so familiar because Mira had worn the perfume when we went out to the club.

Mira was the Antique Burglar.

Frantically, I called Prabhat. I had to ensure my suspicions were right, and I asked him to give me Mira's address. At first, he seemed sceptical, considering I gave him no explanation. However, there was no time for one.

As I made my way to Mira's house, I felt adrenaline coursing through my body. I had done it. I had figured out who the Antique Burglar was.

When I reached her house, I knocked on the door with my gun in my hands. To my surprise, her house was empty. I rechecked every nook and cranny to make sure no one was there.

I was about to leave when I heard music playing from behind me. It was the song from the first card. I clutched my gun and turned around. There I saw a box, a large box. I sat down on a chair and opened it. Inside it was a boatload of cash. Along with it was a letter.

Hi, Venky

It's me, Mira. You're pathetic to think I don't have your phone bugged. Actually, if I'm being honest, I don't. Prabhat's phone is bugged. I've already left, but I never thought you'd come after me even after realizing it's me. After all, I did this for you. Prabhat told me stories about the filthy people at your job and your dream to pursue research. So this is for you. Go follow your dream. Besides, even if you try, you won't find me; so don't waste your time. Anyway, congrats

for piecing it all together, but you're a little too slow. Hope you miss me because I'll miss you.
Xoxo, Mira

As I put the letter down on the table, I thrust my head back and closed my eyes. Oh, how torturous the comments from Ritesh would be the next day!

I figured out who the burglar was, but she slipped through my fingers.

13

HEIST OF LIVES

The officer made his way around town,
Through the narrow streets of the Earth,
Across faces showcasing an overbearing frown,
Contemplating the pennies they're worth.

The baker's dough,
The jeweller's gold,
Both in woe,
Hiding secrets untold.

As he looked around, he saw,
Various participants in a never-ending rat race,
Crushed by something called the law,
Overlooking justice in the name of grace.

FANTASY, REALITY OR DELUSION?

Searching for a means of survival,
Through unethical ways,
Resulting in a state of deprival,
Left with nothing but an endless maze.

As the officer walked further,
The streets grew narrow,
The people looked as if they were lacking fervour,
And a man in the corner was wielding a barrow.

The officer approached the man,
Asking what happened to the town,
That once thrived through every shop it ran,
And people bore a smile, not a frown.

The man looking dim held the officer's hand,
And told him how corporations led the town to its end,
Seized their assets and all of their land,
A loss which no one could ever mend.

The lives of the people suffered a change for the worse,
The happiness on their faces was long gone,
The cheer once related to this town was now a curse,
In the blink of an eye, from dusk to dawn.

HEIST OF LIVES

Their strikes failed with misery,
The wealthy struck us down with knives,
Oh, if this isn't a tragedy!
It is merely *a heist of lives.*

14

RUNAWAY

I was on my way to work, which I despised. The pay was not enough to cover even one-fifth the amount of work they made us do, but then what's the best job a person can get who hasn't gone to college?

As I walked down the narrow alley to my workplace, I saw an old man handing out pamphlets.

'Find a way to escape your life,' he kept telling passers-by. Oh, how I hated such people who sold bullshit to naïve people. As if! If someone had found a way to escape life, I certainly wouldn't be working a minimum-wage job. Instead, I would be sipping drinks on a beach in Hawaii, and everyone around me would be doing so too!

'Hey, old man, do yourself a favour and do

something that doesn't involve scamming people,' I said approaching him.

'Oh, young lady, I am a simple man who comes from nothing. The last thing I would do is scam people who have done nothing wrong. I can really help you escape your life,' he said.

'And how would that happen?' I said snarking at what he told me.

'You don't believe me, do you? Well, now you will,' he said and handed me one of his pamphlets.

The pamphlet was weird. It was a picture of a cluster of galaxies—approximately a hundred—and each galaxy had a name written above it. Some were even marked with special stars that indicated the galaxy's age.

'Just choose one galaxy that you find the prettiest and say its name out loud after thinking about your innermost desires regarding how you want to run away,' he said.

'Okay, old man, and if nothing happens, I'll have at least the satisfaction of proving you wrong.' Sighing, I said the name out loud, 'Whirlpool. See, nothing happ—' I couldn't finish my sentence. I didn't know how to describe it, but I felt like I was melting away. I tried to open my eyes, but they wouldn't budge. I felt like I was floating. At the same time, I felt like I was moving rapidly through a maze-like structure.

RUNAWAY

Suddenly, I felt the urge to open my eyes, and as I did, I saw a bright light at the end of what seemed like a tunnel. When I came to, I saw barren land with barely any trees. But something was off: the ground was purple in colour. I could physically see the wind blowing in front of my face. I smelled ammonia, the same chemical smell I used to identify during our chemistry class at school.

As I tried to pick myself off the ground, my legs wouldn't move. It felt like my ankles were bound by a chain. This is when I started to realize the situation I was in. What had just happened? I started panicking a little.

Just then, I saw someone, another person. It was a tall man, wearing a white T-shirt under blue overalls. He was wearing chunky boots, like the kind you wear when you're going skiing. He had a sledge attached to a rope and was dragging it along over his shoulder. I could barely see his face from this distance.

'HELLOOOO!' I screamed while waving my hands vigorously in the air. He didn't seem to notice.

'HELLO THERE, MAN! PLEASE HELP ME!' I screamed louder and waved my hands with even more vigour. This time, he noticed me. He dropped the rope and started jogging towards me. As he got closer, I could tell he was around thirty years old.

FANTASY, REALITY OR DELUSION?

'HELLO,' he greeted me as he approached me, taking a second to catch his breath.

'Who are you, and what are you doing all the way out here?' he asked me with a stern look on his face.

'Look, man, I don't mean to cause any trouble. I think I got drugged or kidnapped, and someone just dropped me off here. I'm really scared, and I don't know my way back from here. Hell, I don't even know where I am!' I exclaimed as I saw his expression change from stern to concerned.

'What's your name, and where exactly do you live?' he asked lending me a hand to get me up.

'I live near Manhattan. I know my way around the local area, so if I could get to any place nearby, it would be helpful,' I said as I took his hand and tried my best to get up, but my legs still wouldn't budge. As I sat back down after my failed attempt to get up, I saw the man's expression change to shock.

'You're from Manhattan... Were you approached by a man who said he would help you escape?' he said with a most concerned look on his face.

'Indeed, I was! Do you know who he is? If I find out, I swear to God I will...'

'I don't know how to tell you this,' he cut me off. 'You're not on Earth any longer.'

RUNAWAY

'What do you mean I'm not on Earth? Is this some kind of joke? Are you working with that weird man?'

'Your legs.'

'What?' I said confused and scared out of my wits.

'Your legs. You can't feel them, can you? That's why you couldn't get up even after I gave you my hand.'

I stared at him in silence. How could he possibly know that?

'I know how that feels. It happened to me too when I first arrived here. The feeling of being unable to move your legs sucks,' he said.

'What do you mean by "when I first arrived here"? Where am I?' I said, asking a question I did not want to know the answer to.

'You're on a planet called Portia in the Whirlpool Galaxy.'

'Wh...whirlpool?' I stuttered as I tried to process what had happened.

'You mean that old man really sent me to another galaxy? Stop lying. Where am I really?'

'You don't believe me? Fine. I'll prove it to you.'

He picked up a rock from the ground and threw it towards the sky. Suddenly, the sky split open, and I could see what could best be described as multiple celestial bodies in the sky. It was like nothing I had seen before.

It was beautiful but frightening. Was I really on another planet?

'Okay, so you're trying to tell me that the old man actually sent me away?' I said exhaling deeply.

'Yes. I know it's a lot to process, but right now, you have to come with me. If you stay in this atmosphere for too long, you'll die.'

He picked me up in his arms, put me down on his sledge and dragged me along for what felt like ages. The journey was so long that I fell asleep. When I woke up, I was lying on a mattress inside a room, which was similar to those on Earth. I got up, and in doing so, I realized I could now move my legs.

I made my way out of the room and saw a huge space with a large sofa, a TV the size of a theatre screen and a glass wall through which I could see the place I was in. It was nothing like New York. There were no tall buildings, skyscrapers or traffic on the roads; but there were lots of trees. The river flowing from a mountain was so big I could see it from here, which was far away.

'Good morning,' I heard a voice say to my right. It was the man. He was standing in front of a stove in a kitchen that was bigger than my apartment.

'Good morning. Do you mind telling me what that is?' I asked pointing at the mountain.

'Here, drink this,' he said handing me a weird-shaped cup with violet vapours coming out of it. He started walking and signalled with his fingers for me to follow.

With the press of a button, the glass walls adjusted themselves and turned into a balcony. I was awestruck. I smelt the drink he had given me; it seemed like a mix of caramel and cinnamon.

'What's in this?' I asked following him to the railing of the newly formed balcony.

'Easy with the questions. Let me answer your first one. The mountain you see right there was formed a billion years ago, around the same time this planet was formed. It is called Suffran. The river, formed not much later, gave birth to organisms that they call Shufflers. Over time, these Shufflers evolved into a species called the Magicians; they are basically like the humans of this planet. As a civilization, these Magicians are ahead of us humans by at least a million years and speak a very advanced language, but they can also speak every language that exists in the whole universe. On this mountain, besides the river that flows through it, grows a rare plant. This plant can supposedly cure any disease and make any being adapt to even the most filthy surroundings by making them invincible. The only thing it cannot do is immortalize beings. This plant is the foundation of the whole planet. It is sold throughout the galaxy and is very profitable.'

With every word that came out of his mouth, my mind was blown away. To think that people on Earth are stuck contemplating whether we are alone or not while civilizations have progressed so much.

'Why don't they try and contact humans?' I asked curiously.

'The Magicians have a civilization so advanced that they have made escaping from a black hole possible. Their laws of science differ immensely from the ones on Earth. They don't deem humans worthy enough to understand their way of life. It's like a human explaining the meaning of life to an ant; however much you try, it won't ever understand. It's the same with them and us. We can't fathom the extent of their intelligence. I have been here for seven Earth years, and even though they welcomed me with open arms, they never tried to involve me in their business. They provide me with food, technology and whatever else I wish for out of pity.'

All of this was a lot to absorb in such a short time. I chuckled a little in shock.

'What's so funny?' he asked.

'Nothing. It's just hilarious how I've gotten myself

into such a terrible situation. Also, I just realized I never asked your name,' I said.

'It's Marc. What's yours?'

'Estelle. Anyway, imagine how many other people must've fallen for this and ended up in several other galaxies. How does that man do it? Is there no way to go back to Earth?'

'Now that you know such a civilization exists, there is no way they'll let you go back to our planet. As far as the man's concerned, I've learnt over the years that it's best not to poke around too much. I can't do anything about it, so what good would knowing the reason do?'

'You're right. I guess I can't really do much now,' I sighed. The idea of a whole civilization shying away from humans blew my mind. We don't know much about the universe we call home.

My eyes scanned the landscape in front of me, which would end up being my home forever.

∽

Several more people dropped by over the years. We even have our own little mini-civilization here.

I wanted to run away from my boring old life, but I was a little too lucky, so they sent me away to a whole other galaxy. Now I wish I had my boring old life back.

FANTASY, REALITY OR DELUSION?

Always be careful what you wish for, kids, and don't approach strange men in alleyways, or you might end up in another galaxy like me.

15
FANTASY

Our world becomes bleak and preposterous at times, spreading a sense of fatigue. What can humans do to escape but indulge in the world of fantasy, which is the more desirable form of our world? But what happens when the lines between the virtual world and reality get blurred?

Humans tend to desire what they cannot possess. Don't we all sometimes believe that a world full of fairies and mystical objects would be far better than the secret little world we possess? Well, I do.

Today's a lazy day. I had to wake up at 10 a.m. for a class at 12 noon, but I procrastinated until 11.30 a.m. *God, I wish someone could teach me how to be on time,*

FANTASY, REALITY OR DELUSION?

I thought to myself. The class was far more interesting than I thought it would be. I studied a chapter on optics where I learnt about real and virtual images in relation to plane mirrors. My teacher felt the need to point out the fact that a virtual world exists beyond the mirror and that light cannot possibly go beyond the mirror. As if that wasn't obvious already. A virtual world? Seriously? I'm not eight any more. Even though I kind of wish it did, nothing of the sort exists. How nice it would be to have an escape from the real world and have some peace in life. Maybe a world made of pancakes. Yum!

As I sat there daydreaming about having pancakes for lunch, my teacher threw a piece of chalk at me. 'Where is your mind at? Pay attention in class,' my teacher remarked with an annoyed look on her face. 'Miss, if you would stop teaching us about imaginary things, I would certainly be compelled to pay attention in class,' I replied as the bell rang and left with my bag before the teacher could reply to my comment.

'What was that about?' my friend asked as I made my way down the hallway. 'You know all this stupidity about fictional worlds gets to my head. Why does everyone need to make up imaginary stuff to cope with life? It's not like we're little kids any more. I'm sick of it.' I rolled my eyes and walked away from my friend.

I made my way to the washroom and took out my lip gloss. 'Virtual world my foot. Why can't people just accept reality?' I said to myself while applying lip gloss.

But something weird happened. Suddenly, the mirror disintegrated into a liquid, which reminded me of gallium. It startled me. How peculiar! I extended my hand towards it to touch it and felt a force pull me in.

When I came to, I was lying on the bathroom floor. What had just happened? I picked myself up to save myself from the embarrassment that would've been inevitable if someone had walked in on me lying on the ground. I quickly made my way out, but I noticed something weird. Everyone was dressed like pirates.

The school was not actually my school. It was a weird cabin on the beach. I could see a maiden wearing a flowy, white full-sleeved dress with a brown corset on top and a bandana on her head. She ran up to me as soon as she noticed me.

'You must go. You don't belong here. Take this, and find me,' she said handing me a note tied with a ribbon. She signalled me towards the bathroom with a door that stood out against the antique place. I went inside, and the mirror started doing the same thing again. I touched it and was sucked in again. When I came to, I was on the ground again, but this time, my best friend was standing over me. She looked concerned.

'Are you okay? Did you fall? Are you hurt? Do you need me to call someone?' she started asking.

'No, just drop me home, please,' I said.

I felt sick to my stomach like someone had just sucker-punched me in the gut. Who was that woman? Was it all a dream? Was I hallucinating?

As soon as I reached home, I fell on my bed and slept for what felt like an eternity.

I woke up in the morning with a splitting headache, but I was intent on going to school. As I packed my bag, I noticed a note in the water bottle compartment. It was the same one that the maiden had given me. What? Was it real?

When you experience something, it becomes insanely hard to make yourself believe it wasn't real. Maybe it was a dream, a hallucination or a fantasy. But in my heart, I truly believed it wasn't. I had travelled back in time.

I left for school early that morning and went to the same washroom straight away. I stared at the mirror for almost half an hour till the bell rang for my first class. Nothing changed. It was a plain old mirror.

After wasting my time, I decided to finally read the

note. Written on it was a poem in the most beautiful cursive handwriting I had ever seen.

> Oh hey, Oh ho,
> Deep where the sunshine glows,
> Underneath the plaque of night and day,
> Down where the stars dance in the sky.
>
> One step, two steps, three steps towards the evening sun,
> Upon the labyrinth like a frog.
> Do it when the sun burns,
> Beneath the stone of freedom, you may,
> Find where the secret stays.

Oh, hell no, I thought to myself. What have I gotten myself into? And what era is this note from? It looks like the note might turn to dust any second. Curse my mouth because it actually disintegrated into dust. Thankfully, I have a good memory.

My first thought was to ask my best friend to come along with me, but when I told her about the note and time travel, she just gazed at me with an open mouth.

'I know it sounds unbelievable, but trust me, there is a treasure here somewhere. I know it,' I said.

'If you don't believe me, just take a look at this.' I

showed her a copy of the poem I had noted down on a piece of paper.

'Fine. I don't believe you, but I'll help you to make sure you don't do something stupid,' she said.

The whole day in class I kept thinking about what it could mean. I decided it would be smartest to decode the poem if I split it into two paragraphs.

Oh hey, Oh ho,
Deep where the sunshine glows,
Underneath the plaque of night and day,
Down where the stars dance in the sky.

I got it! There was an astronomical observation site downtown that could manually tell time. There were a couple of telescopes located not far from the site, which could be what 'down where the stars dance in the sky' meant.

Before I could decode the second paragraph, it was the end of the school day. My best friend and I decided to decode it after reaching the site. I equipped my bag as though I was leaving for war and walked towards my best friend's house first.

We left around 5 p.m. for the site and reached at 5.30. It was a Friday, so the site was closed to visitors, but we managed to sneak in through the maintenance gate. After sneaking in, we travelled down to where the telescopes were. There were about seven telescopes, and in the middle, there was a plaque directing tourists towards the site, which was what I assumed was mentioned in the poem. I went and stood next to the plaque.

I unfolded the piece of paper with the poem and started decoding the second paragraph.

'One step, two steps, three steps.' Did that mean I had to take three steps? I took three steps in the direction of the sun. It felt a bit stupid considering the next line didn't match.

'Maybe it means you have to take six steps,' my best friend said, pointing at a stone structure a little ahead of me. Of course, how could I be so blind!?!

I proceeded to walk towards it. When I examined it closely, I realized that the small stone-like structure had a labyrinth drawn on it.

Now, the poem said, 'Upon the labyrinth like a frog', so I jumped onto the small structure with all my might. Nothing happened. All this wordplay was making me lose my mind.

I tried to use my brain, and then the next line came into play. 'Do it when the sun burns.' Maybe it meant when the sun sets.

So we waited and waited and waited. We waited

till the sun was setting, and again, I jumped onto the structure with all my might.

Suddenly, the small structure started shaking violently. The ground beside the structure started to crumble and revealed a chest. The stone chest had a weird parrot design on it. It was about six feet wide and four feet tall.

The chest was locked by another stone with a maze imprinted on it. A small steel ball was trapped in the middle of the maze. 'The stone of freedom.' It meant I had to solve the maze and free the ball.

It took me about twenty minutes to free the ball. By then, the sun had almost set, and we were starting to lose daylight.

As soon as I freed the ball, the chest sprung open. A nasty odour reached our nostrils. Inside the chest was a skeleton. Around the skeleton lay multiple bugs, insects and gold. Pure gold. I gasped. I was in awe and horrified at the same time. Whose skeleton was this?

That is when I remembered the maiden's words, 'Take this and find me.' Maybe it was her skeleton.

As I extended my hand to pick up the gold, it disintegrated. All of it crumbled to dust: the gold, the skeleton and the chest. I couldn't believe my eyes. How was any of this even possible? My heart sank. We made a groundbreaking discovery but had nothing to show for it.

FANTASY, REALITY OR DELUSION?

All of a sudden, I had a piercing pain in my head and fell to the ground. When I awoke, my best friend was standing over me asking if I was okay. I was back in my school's washroom, lying on the floor.

Since then, I have tried multiple times to find the treasure. My best friend has no recollection of ever going to the site with me. It was real. I know it. It felt so real. But how do I prove something I have no physical evidence of? My family thinks I made it up as an escape from my everyday life, as if I travelled into the very 'virtual world' whose idea I opposed.

Oh, dear maiden, why choose me?

Now only you and I know that what's a fantasy to them is a reality I lived.